MISTER NOBODY

Margaret Moon

Illustrated by Virginia Barrett

Momentum
Mister Nobody

First published in Great Britain in 1998 by

Folens Publishers
Albert House
Apex Business Centre
Boscombe Road
Dunstable
Beds LU5 4RL

© 1998 Momentum developed by Barrie Publishing Pty Limited
Suite 513, 89 High St, Kew, Vic 3101, Australia

Margaret Moon hereby asserts her moral right to be identified as
the author of this work in accordance with the Copyright, Designs
and Patents Act 1988.
© 1998 Folens Ltd. on behalf of the author.
Illustrations copyright Virginia Barrett

British Library Cataloguing in Publication Data.
A Catalogue record for this book is available from the British
Library

ISBN 1 86202 388 3

Designed by Pauline McClenahan
Printed in Singapore by PH Productions Pte Ltd

Michael had a very special friend. His name was Mister.

Michael's parents always asked him, "Mister who?"

Michael always answered, "Mister Nobody."

You see, Mister was invisible to everyone but Michael.

One day, Michael and Mister were playing in the back garden with Woofer, Michael's dog. It was a very hot day so they turned on the hose. All of a sudden, Mister grabbed the hose from Michael and sprayed it all over the side of the house.

"Oh, no!" said Michael.

His bedroom window was open and his
dinosaur curtains were dripping wet. Mister
dropped the hose as Michael's mother came
rushing out of the house. She saw the hose
wriggling around on the ground like a long
green snake.

"It wasn't me!" Michael shouted excitedly.
"It was Mister!"

"Then you can take Mister inside and make
sure he cleans up the mess."

The carpet was soaked.

The wardrobe door was open and Michael's clothes were dripping.

Michael got a sponge and began to clean up the water. He was glad he was wearing his boots.

That night, when Michael's dad came to say good night, Michael said, "Could you leave the light on in the hall, please?"

"Sure," said his dad. "Are you scared?"

"No, but Mister is," said Michael.

Mister thought that the wardrobe looked scary when the door was left open at night. Michael always made sure that the doors were closed, but tonight the doors were propped open so everything could dry out.

Michael woke up in the middle of the night to find Mister sitting on the end of his bed.

"What's the matter?" asked Michael.

"I thought I heard a thumping noise in the wardrobe," said Mister. "Could you go and look? Please?"

Michael knew that Mister was too afraid to look in the wardrobe.

So Michael put one foot out on the damp floor. Slowly he put out his other foot. Mister gave him a little push from behind.

"Go on," Mister whispered, and he jumped under the covers.

Michael took a deep breath and crept forward. He was glad that Mister could not see how scared he really was. Suddenly a huge shadow fell across the floor. The shadow had long, long legs and great dangling arms like an ape. Michael froze.

"What are you doing out of bed?" asked Michael's dad as he switched on the light. The shadow disappeared.

"Mister thought he heard a funny noise in the wardrobe," Michael answered.

"Together he and his dad looked inside. Woofer lay curled up in the wardrobe. He looked up and started wagging his tail. His tail went *Thump, thump, thump*.

"Come out of there, Woofer," said Michael's dad.

Michael hugged his dad and hopped back into bed. He was sure Mister would be happy now that he knew they were safe.

Now they could both go back to sleep.